The Orchard Book of
Love and
Friendship

For Teresa and James
G.M

For David, Clara, Elly and Joe
J.R.

Orchard Books
96 Leonard Street, London EC2A 4XD
Orchard Books Australia
14 Mars Road, Lane Cove, NSW 2066
First published in Great Britain in 2000
ISBN 1 86039 493 0
Text © Geraldine McCaughrean 2000
Illustrations © Jane Ray 2000
The rights of Geraldine McCaughrean to be identified as the author and
Jane Ray to be identified as the illustrator have been
asserted by them in accordance with the
Copyright, Designs and Patents Act, 1988.
A CIP catalogue record for this book is available from the British Library
1 3 5 7 9 10 8 6 4 2
Printed in Singapore

The Orchard Book of
Love and Friendship

Geraldine
McCaughrean

Jane
Ray

 ORCHARD BOOKS

Contents

The First Family

The world God made is large and irregular. And what with the wide-washing oceans, and jumbling of thornbushes, and dense forest groves, not everything in it is easily found. At the very beginning, when only three people lived on all the Earth, they did not even know of each other's existence. And though it was not the will of God, they were all three very lonely.

First Man Monday was so lonely that he carved a log of wood: a hand, a foot, a face. He carved the likeness of a woman (though he had never seen one), and was more than pleased with the result. Polishing it with a knot of grass, he propped it against his house.

"Good," he said, cleaning his chisel, and running his eye over the arm, the leg, the breast. "Excellent."

As the days passed, and the woodcarver came and went, he grew more and more fond of his handiwork. "Lovely," he would say as he passed by. "Quite beautiful!" And he ran his fingertips over the forehead, the little flat nose.

 In fact it gave him such joy that he moved it into the forest clearing where he could see it while he worked, chopping wood. The sight of the wooden woman gave him an ache now, in his chest: not unpleasant, rather a kind of cramping pleasure. He called her Sela, and chattered away to her while he worked, so that he no longer felt so lonely; no, hardly at all.

But with leaving his statue out there in the open, where anyone might see it who chanced by, one early world dawn Second Man Tuesday came by while First Man Monday was still in bed.

When he saw the carving, the sight of it struck him like a spear in the heart, and he reeled with emotion.

"Oh, you beautiful thing!" he cried, and began to run to and fro in wild excitement, clumsily, eagerly, only half knowing what he was doing. He took off his cloak and wrapped it around the statue, so that it should not be naked. He picked flowers for her, and made a coronet of blossom for her head. He found shells on the beach, and made necklaces for her throat, and lit a fire

nearby to keep her warm. Further and further afield he went, in search of feathers and seeds and anything he could find to adorn his beautiful statue. For he assumed, since God had placed it in his path, that the statue was intended for him.

While he was away, the smoke of the fire caught the eye of First Woman Wednesday, and she was curious to see where it came from.

When she entered the clearing and saw the statue all decked and adorned and as gleaming as a moonlit sea, she rushed over to it, arms wide, grin wider.

"Another person! A companion! A friend for me in my loneliness. Oh God be praised!" But when she kissed the cheek it was cold, and when she clasped the hand, it was stiff. Only wood. No words in the mouth, no hearing in the ears, no sight in the two ebony eyes.

Woman Wednesday's disappointment was terrible. Her arm embracing the carving, she slid down to her knees. "Oh, if only you had life, you lovely girl! If only I could have you for a friend, and not live lonely any more on this big, big world!"

The leaves on the trees trembled. The sea licked the shore into new shape.

The woman picked up the statue – it took all her strength – and carried it as far as she was able, down to the sea-shore where she lived. By the time she got there, she was tired out, and lay down on the sand, her arms round the beautiful statue, her cheek pressed against its ebony hair.

And the sea trembled and the leaves on the trees lapped up the daylight and night fell.

In the morning, the woodman, Man Monday, set out to work as usual. But when he reached the clearing, his beloved carving was gone. Howling with rage, he followed the thief's trail through the bush.

Young Man Tuesday, back from diving for pearls on the far-off oyster beds, found his beloved statue gone. Roaring with anguish, he followed the well trampled trail through the bush and down to the sea.

Woman Wednesday, sleeping on the beach, was woken by two men bursting out of the trees, running towards her, yelling and shaking their fists. Startling enough, to find that she was not alone in the world. More startling still to find that her arms were full of girl.

The ebony statue was no more. Thanks to the woman's prayer, it had turned into real flesh and blood – and hair and smile and talk. And if she had been beautiful before, now Sela was lovely enough to break the ice off Antarctica, the peaks off the Pyrenees.

"She's mine!" said Man Monday, seizing hold of her hand. "I love her!"

"She's mine!" said young Man Tuesday, pummelling the woodcarver in the back. "I love her!"

"She's mine!" said Woman Wednesday, biting their ankles and fingers and clinging tight to the girl. "I love her!"

"Shall we not ask God?" whispered Sela, whose hair was being severely pulled and whose clothes were being torn.

So they asked God, and God said this, while the sea held its breath,

and the trees held still their leaves:

"You, Monday, shall be the girl's father, because she was your idea."

"Mine, as I said!" declared Monday proudly.

"You, Wednesday, shall be the girl's mother," said God, "because you gave her life."

"Mine!" said Wednesday with a happy sigh. "I knew it."

"And you, Tuesday, shall be the girl's husband, because you provided for her and took care of her in every way."

"Oh!" exclaimed Tuesday, and clasping both hands over his heart swooned quietly away in an ecstasy of happiness.

"Oh!" said Sela, and immediately began to look after her husband – fetching him water, cooking him fish, fanning his face with a palm leaf.

Monday helped Wednesday to her feet, and brushed the sand out of her hair. There was a cold wind blowing out to sea, so he let her share his cloak.

And do you know? Although that first family were still alone on the surface of a big, big world, they did not feel so lonely any more. And what with children and grandchildren, younglings and babies, the world filled up in no time, no time at all. Too much, God sometimes thinks, as He tries to get some shut-eye.

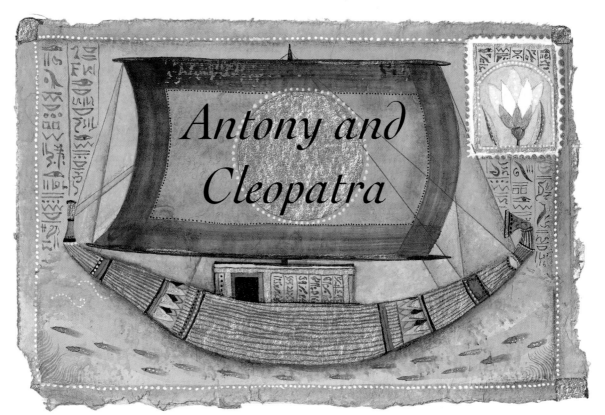

Antony and Cleopatra

In the days when the Roman empire reached out into every corner of the world, Marcus Antonius took it upon himself to visit the golden territories of Egypt. He had taken power in Rome, and now Egypt was his, and everything in it.

Roman generals had been there before, of course. They had come home speaking of fabulous wealth, of sumptuous luxury but above all they had come home speaking of Queen Cleopatra. They said she was the most beautiful woman in the world. They said she was the most cunning. Like a Nile snake she could slither her way into a man's heart and fasten so tightly on it that nothing but death could set him free.

Antony saw no danger to his own heart, though. After all, Cleopatra was no longer young, and Antony already had a wife. He was simply going to visit a distant corner of his empire, to take the measure of its conquered queen.

The first time he saw her, she arrived aboard a golden barge aswarm with cupids, billowing with scented sails. The sight of her sank deep into every heart, just as she had meant it to. "A fine piece of theatre," muttered Antony, but his heart was beating faster, and he felt a kind of magic settle on his eyelids. No sooner did their eyes meet, than Love robbed them both of their reason. Cleopatra and Antony were all in all to one another.

Rome and home dwindled to nothing in Antony's reckoning. The sweetness he tasted on Cleopatra's lips robbed him of all desire to leave Egypt. She loved him and he loved her. Where is the harm in True Love? None – except that Antony already had a wife in Rome, and Rome could not spare its ruler and its greatest general.

In his heart of hearts, Antony knew he was needed elsewhere. Part of him wanted to break free. But it took a letter from home to wake him like a slap in the face.

"Fulvia is dead," he read aloud, the letter trembling in his hand.

"Your wife?" Cleopatra uncurled like a cat.

"She tried to take power in Rome. People are saying I was in league with her! The city is in turmoil! I must get back there! I must!"

Cleopatra let him go with hardly a murmur. After all, he swore to return as soon as he could, and when he returned, he would be a widower, a single man, free to marry. After he had gone, she passed the slow, dreary days daydreaming and writing love letters, planning for the day she and Antony would be together again.

Lion-like, Antony roared back into Rome, putting down rebellion, scotching the rumours, winning back the crowds who swarmed to see him.

But Antony, for all his great power, did not rule Rome single-handed. He shared the position of emperor with another man – Octavius – and never were two men more different in nature. Octavius was a sober puritan. He despised Antony for his 'little Egyptian romance'. It had ruined any friendship which had ever existed between them. But for the country's sake, these 'brother-emperors' had to try and get along.

"If only there were some bond which would bind us together in genuine brotherhood!" mused Octavius, watching Antony with a cold, glittering eye.

Meanwhile Cleopatra dreamed the days away in Egypt, desert-thirsty for news of Antony. Any day now, he would surely return to Egypt and marry her. Then all of a sudden, news! A dust-covered, breathless, pale-faced runner carrying a letter with Antony's seal upon it. News of Antony! News of what? Marriage?

Antony had married Octavius' sister.

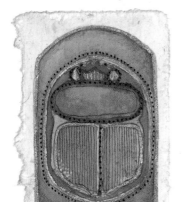

It was a political alliance, of course: a public show of unity between Octavius and Antony, to stabilise a tricky political situation back in Rome. But Cleopatra did not see it in that light. She slumped back in her Egyptian throne and howled like a dog; howled and

snarled and snapped at all who came near.

She sent messengers of her own to find out about Octavia. There was gold for anyone who came back swearing Octavia was squat, plain, ageing, cold – unlovable. But even so she only half believed the words her messengers dutifully spoke to her.

She need not have worried. Octavia was neither squat nor plain, but she was not the woman to drive Cleopatra out of Antony's dreams at night. A respectable, loveless, arranged marriage could not compare with his days and nights on the Nile. Within weeks, Antony was yearning for his Egyptian Queen again. He could not keep away.

Secretly Octavius Caesar was itching for an excuse to make war on Antony. He took the greatest delight in breaking the news to his sister – poor unloved Octavia – that Antony had run off back to Egypt – to Cleopatra. "They have children now, you know? He's crowning them 'Kings of the Earth', squandering Roman treasure on them and on that Nile crocodile." Though he made great show of sympathising with his miserable, wronged sister, secretly her tears scalded him with delight. For now he had his excuse. Now he could declare war on Antony! And that was one step from grasping sole government of the world. No more power-sharing: Octavius meant to have it all.

What did Cleopatra care? Antony was with her once more, and her Antony trailed comets and stars from his hairs' end. He could defeat any enemy who marched against him, couldn't he? He could rule the world alone, from an Egyptian throne! Amid the hot splendour of Egypt, where the sun shines too brightly

for a man to fully open his eyes, Antony began to believe it too. He began to believe all that Cleopatra said of him, and to behave as if he were invincible.

The army he mustered was made up of peasants and labourers, and yet when Octavius sent a fleet against him, Antony determined to fight him at sea.

"Don't do it, master," pleaded his lieutenant. "His ships are light and quick – yours are great unwieldy hulks, and your men are no sailors!"

"But I have sixty galleys," boasted Cleopatra airily, as if that made for an invincible navy. Antony's officers stood about open-mouthed with amazement that their commander should let himself be misled by this woman.

Their fears were well grounded. In the middle of the battle, Cleopatra lost her nerve and fled, her sixty galleys ploughing in among Antony's ships and away. Chaos followed on confusion. Worst of all, Antony, his heartstrings tied tight to Cleopatra's rudder, followed after her like a little broken sea anchor. It was a rout.

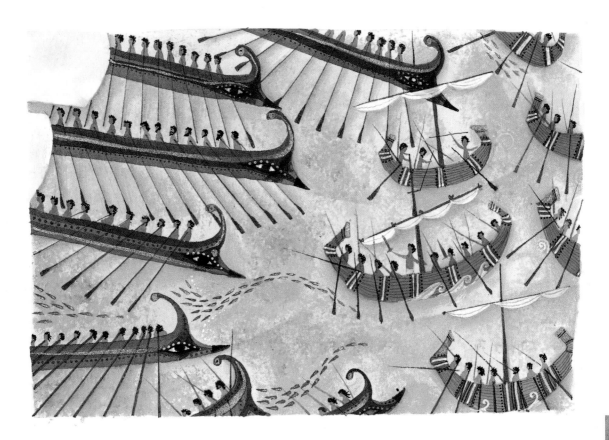

Afterwards, Antony's anger with Cleopatra was only surpassed by his disgust with himself. His reputation, honour, self-respect were in ruins. Like an animal caught in a trap, he writhed to break free of his obsessive love — but could not. Cleopatra had only to cry for him to forgive her everything. She had only to kiss him for his courage and insane confidence to recover.

"Octavius may defeat me on the sea. Does he really suppose he can beat me on dry land?" Everything seemed possible to Antony, because Cleopatra believed in him.

The battles raged on, one fusing into the next. Everything was muddle and misunderstandings. A trick of the light — that blinding, Egyptian sunlight — and Antony thought he saw Cleopatra's cohorts surrendering to the enemy.

What, then, had Cleopatra betrayed him? The thought pitched him into such an envious, insane rage that Cleopatra had to run for her life.

"To the monument! To the monument!" Cleopatra shrieked to her waiting women. "He's mad! He'll kill us all!" Over the stinging heat of midday sand they ran, to the tiny door and up the pitch-black stairs which wound upwards inside a gigantic statue of a sphinx. Couched on perpetual guard beside the palace, the Sphinx raised up its carved head half as high as the sun

and snarled at the sea.

Between its paws, in a chamber high up above the surrounding desert, Cleopatra bewailed the loss of Antony's love. "How shall I bring him to his senses, women? How can I make him love me again?"

And, in her panic, she tried one last, desperate trick. "Tell him I've died of grief! Then he'll be sorry! Then he'll forgive me!"

What did she think he would do, this man maddened by defeat? Too late it dawned on her what effect her words would really have on Antony. She sent a second message, declaring her undying, deathless love, and she told the messenger: "Go quickly. There's a coldness here, over my heart. I'm afraid, suddenly. Run!"

Too late. The messenger found an Antony greatly changed. One shoulder shrugged against a wall, his knees drawn up to his chest, he lay passively in a pool of red, a blood-stained sword drawn and in his hand. The smile on his face was oddly twisted.

"I've conquered a million men in battle," he whispered. "Could I not manage to kill myself?" He had botched his own suicide, left himself stranded between life and death.

His men carried him to the monument – to the Sphinx. The little door was locked, the key thrown away into the darkness and lost. It was necessary

to haul up Antony with scarves and ropes, so that he could breathe his last in the arms of Cleopatra.

She felt his soul slip away between her fingers as easily as desert sand – and when it was gone, there was nothing left in the world of the smallest consequence to her.

"Antony dead?" The words jarred the breath out of Octavius like a sword blow. Real tears sprang to his eyes, for all he had wanted Antony's downfall. Like Cleopatra, he had thought Antony immortal, indestructible, too large for death to swallow without choking. Together, the two of them had held the round world. If one of them could fall, then so could the other. Antony beckoned Octavius from beyond the grave, where all the world's most powerful men count for nothing.

Nothing. There was nothing either admirable or extraordinary left in Cleopatra's world. So it was with only half an ear that she listened to Octavius calling up to her from the foot of the monument: "Give yourself up! You have nothing to fear!" His promises echoed hollow off the great stone Sphinx.

Common sense told Cleopatra that if Octavius captured her, he would parade his conquered 'Egyptian' through the streets of Rome and murder all her children. Cleopatra made her decision. She would rob Octavius of any such spiteful victory. She would die, as Antony had died, and the two of them would be together once and for all.

Cleopatra robed herself in queenly splendour and, seated between the giant paws of the impassive Sphinx, laid a venomous Nile asp to her breast. Like a baby she cradled it. Several moments passed in waiting for the snake to bite.

Death came softly, without pain, and her waiting women followed her willingly along the same path – into the shady lotus orchards of the Afterlife. They could almost hear ahead of them the murmuring voices of lovers reunited.

Hero and Leander

Hero was made for Love. That is to say, she was made for the goddess of Love – for Venus – apprenticed into the priesthood of Venus, so that her days were spent tending the altars and sacred lamps in a temple on the shores of the Hellespont.

Lovers gazing into each other's eyes, shy lonely boys, merry widows, the parents of gawky, unappealing daughters came, from morning till night, hoping to win the help of the goddess of Love and the gift of lasting happiness. Hero saw them all come and go, saw many of their wishes granted, saw many a bride place her wedding bouquet at the feet of Venus' statue as a thanksgiving. But for Hero there was to be no such happy ending. She was a priestess in the Temple of Venus, and priestesses do not marry, do not dance or chatter or keep company with young men. Their life has been dedicated to the gods. Hero's days were spent in the temple, and her nights passed in a tall tower behind it, hard against the seashore, as solitary as any lighthouse keeper. She was not unhappy. At night she could hear the sea breathe in and out, in and out, like someone beside her in the dark.

But just as the light of a lighthouse carries across water, so word of Hero's beauty spread far and wide. Soon, among the sweethearts and parents and lovelorn boys, there came tourists too, sightseers anxious to see the beautiful priestess Hero.

Leander was one. On the annual festival of Venus, he sailed from his home in Abydus across the Hellespont to Sestus to pay homage at the Temple of the

goddess of Love. But though he brought white lilies to lay at the statue's feet, and said his prayers like a devout worshipper, his eyes were really on the priestess, moving among the festival-goers like a swan through seaweed. He looked – and suddenly all his prayers were to have her. Hero saw him looking at her, and though her face flushed scarlet, she did not look away.

High on her plinth, Venus saw the look which passed between Hero and Leander, and though she could be a jealous goddess at times, she recognised the spark of True Love, and she blessed it. Worshippers that festival day swore they had heard the vast white statue sigh a sigh tender with compassion.

Leander presented his lilies to the priestess. "I must see you – alone!" he whispered from among the white flower trumpets.

"That cannot be!" Hero whispered back. "I am forbidden to speak alone with young men."

But Leander would not be put off. "I shall come to you tonight. In your tower."

"No! You'll be seen!"

"Not if I swim across." And he laughed.

"Swim the Hellespont? It can't be done!"

"For you, I can do anything."

She let her eyes drop to his strong shoulders, his broad chest. He might just do it, too. But after dark, and out at sea, it is easy to lose direction.

"I'll light a torch to guide you," she said.

Then a chanting, dancing procession passed between them, and they were separated by the music and celebration of the festival.

That night, Hero stood on the roof of her seaward-facing tower, and looked out across the Hellespont. It is only a strip of salt water – narrow enough, heaven knows, in comparison with the two seas it joins. And yet it is enough to separate two continents, two races, two empires and all but the most desperate lovers. That night it lay calm and luminous, flecked with colours from the setting sun. She almost felt she could swim it herself. But oh! the far shore was so indistinct. Would Leander truly swim all that way? Or had he simply been boasting?

The purple sea darkened to black. Hero fetched a tarry torch and lit it. It flared up brightly and burned with a steady glare.

Three miles off, on the beach below the town of Abydus, Leander was already wading knee-deep in the warm summer water, holding his shoes, waiting for the signal. Would Hero really light a flare to guide him, or would she have thought better by now of his improper proposal? When he saw the prickle of light on the horizon, he flung his shoes ashore and plunged underwater. The sea held no fears for him, and tonight such a fire burned within him that he barely noticed

how the deep water was colder than the shallow, how the currents tugged on him and the salt caked his hair. He swam and he swam till the land behind him was as far off as the land ahead, and there was no point in turning back.

Then his muscles began to ache, and the water to slop in at his mouth and nose. His swimming grew ragged, and the current dragged him further off course. But Leander fixed his eyes on that flickering light and saw in it Hero's face, watching for him, believing in him, willing him to succeed.

Finally, he began to flounder and roll. Perhaps, after all, he had overestimated his strength, his stamina, his bravery.

Then his dangling feet scraped on rocks, and he found himself within his depth, able to stagger ashore. And before he had even reached the beach, he heard Hero splashing into the water and felt her arms enfolding his head. They kissed beneath the seventh wave. They kissed upon the shore. They kissed on the staircase of her lonely tower, and on its roof.

Very little but kisses passed between them that first night – not words, not vows, not compliments. And yet by dawn they knew each other better than the best of friends.

Leander barely noticed the effort of swimming home again. He barely felt his tiredness next day, or the ache of his weary muscles. By dusk he was ready to plunge again into the sparkling Hellespont and cross over to Hero.

All summer long he plied the Dardanelles like a three-sail ferry. To and fro he swam, across the channel, fixing his course by the flicker of torchlight burning on Hero's tower. Even under the drenching rain of autumn, when the downpour flattened the ocean round him, he still kept his nightly tryst. Days would have been insupportable to both of them, if they had not the nights in prospect, the comfort of each other's arms.

Winter comes round the corner of Asia like a bully looking for a fight. It rolls up the blue-green summer surface like a worn rug, pocketing spume and waterspouts. Now, instead of red sunsets brightening Leander's evening vigil, the lovers woke to red dawns overhead.

"Don't come tonight," said Hero, braiding her hair with her back turned to Leander.

"Why not? Are you tired of me already?"

She threw up her hands, and her braids unravelled. "Of course not! I shall be as empty as a broken jug. But you mustn't cross over tonight. There's a storm coming. It's too dangerous."

"I'd like to see the storm that could stop me!" Leander bragged, though he could not help but know that the water was growing colder every day, rougher every time he swam through it.

"I shan't light a flame tonight," said Hero.

"Then you can't risk your life. How do you think

I would feel if…"

"I shall come anyway!" said Leander, brushing aside her thoughts before she could speak them out loud. They both of them knew what he risked every night, though neither had ever spoken of it, or let it cloud their sunny bliss.

"Say you won't! Don't frighten me saying that! We can be patient just one day, can't we? The storm will be all blown out tomorrow." And she clung so tightly round his neck that at last she wrung from him a promise that he would not risk the stormy sea.

But as he turned to go, she thought she saw such a mischievous twinkle in his eye that she could not afterwards be sure, not absolutely sure, what he had decided to do.

All next day she was in a torment of anxiety. Surely he would not try.

The sea was piling up against the rocks below her tower so that there was no beach left but for a few large boulders washed with foam. The sky was the colour of old bruises, the seagulls falling away to the left and right as though their hearts were failing.

Without the prospect of seeing her lover, Hero was filled with weariness and gloomy foreboding. Now that the winter had come, how many other nights would they have to spend apart? And perhaps if he could not see her, Leander would forget her – see some other face which captured his imagination. Perhaps the sea which separated them would be large enough, after all, to extinguish their love.

And had he meant his promise? Would he keep it? Or would he keep the other promise he had made her a thousand times – never to let a night pass without holding her in his arms? Hero did not know which thought appalled her more: that he would try to come, or that he would not. The rising storm set the temple doors banging, and made the lemon trees scratch against the walls. A tedious grey rain swept in.

"He won't come. He couldn't possibly come," Hero told herself watching the rain trickle off the rusty bracket where her torch usually burned. "If I light a flame, he will see it and think that I need him, and come to me, come what may."

The thunder bellowed at her like a rampaging bull.

"And yet if he does try to come, and I haven't lit a flame, he'll be lost out there, with nothing to guide him!"

From that moment, she knew no peace of mind. Indecision stung her like hornets. She fetched out the torch. She carried it back inside. She battened it to the wall, and then could not put light to it for the sheeting rain, the howling wind.

Not three miles away, Leander, swamped by a gigantic wave, turned for the shore again, defeated. Hero would understand. She did not, after all, expect him. Dragging himself ashore on the beach below Abydus, chilled to the marrow and disgusted at his feebleness, he turned to bid a silent farewell to Hero, blowing her a salt-wet kiss.

And there – like a fragment of lightning snagged on the far shore – flickered Hero's

beckoning light. She did after all expect him to cross over. And if she believed he could do it, that is what he would do! Nothing would stop him.

He plunged into the sea like a cormorant, and it threw him almost as high as the racing clouds. The sea ran at him from north, south, east and west, and if it had not been for that glimmer of light, he would have lost all sense of direction.

On top of her tower, Hero cursed the storm. The bully wind shoved her to right and left, and the rain doused her from head to foot, so that her hair was pasted to her dress and her dress to her skin. She shivered uncontrollably. But like an eagle sheltering its eggs from the tempest, she made wings of her sodden cloak and spread it behind her, sheltering the torch from the wind. If it were to go out now! She must not let it. It must burn as bright and constant as her love for Leander. Leander might be depending on it, might have his eye fixed on it at that very moment.

His hands were cold past feeling, his ribs kicked in by the stampeding sea. His stomach was full of saltwater, and his strength all but gone. But it could

not be far now, not very much further. He peered through the spindrift for the pale, impermanent flicker, for his guiding light.

Nothing. He saw only blackness – a few spiteful stars through a tear in the clouds, but of land or lights nothing. The wave dropped him sickeningly into a trough of cold, black water, but not so deep as despair dropped him: alone, lost, foundering, in the pitiless sea.

By creeping, double-over, her body almost forming a letter O, Hero managed to fetch a lighted candle up the steps to the roof and over to the smoking, sodden torch. Despite her wet flapping hair, her frozen hands, Hero succeeded in re-lighting the tarry beacon and this time she was able to keep her flame alive, though by morning she was half dead with cold.

No Leander came. "I knew he would not," she told herself. "I hoped he would not." The storm had blown itself out, and the coming day promised a renewed stint of summer, with a clear blue sky and high white clouds, though the sea was still running high. "He will come tonight," she thought. "Tonight it will be safe." And she lingered at the top of her tower savouring the thought of him, before it was time to descend to the temple and open the doors.

Below her the sea seethed up the beach, flowing round the base of the tower in long dark swathes brocaded with broken foam. Here, a family of gulls were riding the swell, there a seal or sea otter rolled in the surf.

Or was it? Are the faces of sea otters so pale? Are their limbs so long? Do they rest their heads on the sea's surface as though it were a pillow?

Leander's drowned body floated so peacefully on the sea, betraying no trace of the struggle which had gone before. The morning light was so pure that Hero could see every detail of his face, every strand of hair swashing loose about his head. She leaned over the parapet and stretched out a hand, as if even from that great height she could brush the hair out of his eyes.

She did not lean out too far. She did not trip. She stepped quite deliberately out into open air, into thin air. Far below, the sea was waiting to bear her up, as it bore Leander on its back. Like the halcyon birds which build their nests on the sea's waves, she and Leander would inhabit, from now on, the tidal world of water and fishes, of laughing bubbles and the green, eternal peace of the great deeps.

Unforgivable

Here, Gelert! Here, boy! To heel! Come, Gelert, come!"

Prince Llewellyn called and whistled, but his wolfhound did not come. A dozen other dogs milled and boiled around his horse's legs, yelping and baying, their breath smoky in the cold air. But he did not want to set off without Gelert, his best, his favourite dog. Gelert was quicker than any dog he had ever owned. He had such a nose that he could follow a boar or a stag through a mountain stream or a field of pigs. He could bound tirelessly through snowdrifts shoulder high, and his ear was always listening for a word, the breath of a word from his master. Most of all, he was a friend to Llewellyn, and he was reluctant to go hunting without his best friend at his side.

Still, Llewellyn called, and Gelert did not come, so the Prince was obliged to amble out of the castle yard with the remainder of his dogs. The weather was bitter. In these remote parts, a boar or a stag meant feasting in a time of hunger, but the daylight hours were short, and there was no time to waste.

The whole landscape looked hungry – the trees mere skeletons of their summer selves, the mountains pale with snow. Wolves were getting bolder every day, creeping down closer and closer to human habitation to snatch at bones in the litter. But winter could not cast its usual gloom over Llewellyn. He was a happy man. His newborn son and heir was strong and healthy and the light of his father's eye. As Llewellyn rode he was imagining how it would be to ride to hounds with his son, his little Dafyd at his side.

On the way home, he was perished. The castle was a welcome sight, with its prospect of a blazing fire and a hot supper. And best of all was the sight of Gelert – that brindled, rangy Irish wolfhound – bounding out across the drawbridge to meet him. Dear dog, splendid dog, excellent Gelert.

There was something strange, though, about his stride – something crumpled and awkward. And there was something strange about his muzzle, normally so clean and grey. The whiskers round his mouth were all slicked down and his nose gleamed with some sticky redness. Blood. The paw that lifted to pat at Llewellyn's stirrup was clarted too with blood.

Somewhere inside Llewellyn's chest a door banged which jarred his whole being. He tried to put the thought out of his mind, but it thrust itself at him, glaring, unignorable. Flinging himself off his horse, he ran for the living apartments across the yard, his boots slipping on the icy flagstones, his fingers grazing the wall. There was no need to unlatch the door; it was already ajar. He slammed it open, and the sight of the whole large room crammed itself into his brain within a single second.

The hangings were all pulled down, the tapestries ripped from the wall. The metal grate had spilled its ashes, and the log basket was overturned. Little Dafyd's cradle lay on its side, empty. And the blood. Oh God, the blood. There was blood on the rush mat, and on the settle. There was blood on the hearth and on the blankets spilled from the upturned cot. There was blood on Gelert's fur and snout as he leapt up to lick his master's face affectionately.

Llewellyn uttered a cry that was barely human in its desolation. "Fiend! Brute! Devil!" he screamed, throwing his dog away from him as he would the Devil himself. "What, did you think to have all my love to yourself, you hell-hound? Well here's the hate you earned, you vile, murdering beast!"

Out came his sword, and he jabbed and slashed and hacked at his dog, till it was no more than a motionless heap of bloody fur at his feet. And all the while he screamed his hatred at this Gelert, this mad, rabid brute which, out of jealousy or some base animal wolfish instinct had mauled and eaten his little baby son.

It was not until he fell exhausted and sobbing to his knees

that he heard it — a feeble, mewing squawk. He thought he must be imagining it, but no. He turned over the cradle. Nothing. He turned over the log basket and the previously muffled noise burst upwards into his face: a baby's crying.

There lay Dafyd, shaking his little fists, as if in wrath at Llewellyn's stupidity.

There was another noise, too — the shuddering last sigh of something lying hidden by the fallen door-curtain. It was so big Llewellyn could hardly believe he had missed seeing it — a massive wolf, ripped and torn by a hundred bites, but as peaceful in death as a dreaming dog.

For an hour Gelert had fought this intruder into the castle in search of easy meat. Crashing against the furniture, pausing neither for breath nor to lick their wounds, the two had pitted themselves to fight to the death over the morsel of life in the cradle. The wolf had starvation to goad it on; Gelert had love — bottomless, devoted, dogged, inexhaustible love for his master and his master's defenceless little child. It was his place in life to defend the loved ones of Llewellyn, and he had defended them with his life.

The door opened which led to the winding stair, and Llewellyn's wife came in. She saw her husband holding their child, barely larger than his two big hands. And she saw the shape of Gelert with the sword still lying bloody across his back.

"What have you done?" she asked.

He looked back at her with a face aghast with guilt. "The unforgivable," he said. "I have done the unforgivable. I have killed my friend because I didn't trust him. I have killed him for saving my son's life."

He thrust the baby into her arms, and picked up the dog instead – so much larger a load that he could barely do it. But he carried Gelert to the door, and fresh snow whirled in as he opened it. "Where are you going?" asked his wife.

"To bury him as befits a friend," said Prince Llewellyn.

He raised a great pile of rocks and stones – a cairn which rose up out of the barren landscape like some prehistoric barrow, burial place of warrior or king. For day after day, in the bitter cold, he went to and fro, lifting the rocks and laboriously carrying them to the cairn. His neighbours marvelled to see it. They marvelled, too, to hear what the dog had done, and wept with Llewellyn to hear how Gelert had been repaid for his devotion.

Whenever he forgot for a few hours, the sight of that cairn would reproach him with the memory. At night, from the window of the room, it looked like a giant dog sleeping curled up in the moonlight. But in as much as he was able, the Prince did reward his faithful hound for the service it had done him. For he made Gelert the most famous dog in all Wales. And, while he had breath still to whistle and to ride out alone in the wild and lonely places, he went on calling and whistling to Gelert's spirit, to Gelert's free-ranging soul.

Tristan and Isolde

*T*welve Cornish maidens and twelve Cornish men: that was the price of peace. Across the ocean in Ireland, King Aengus of Munster demanded tribute from all the petty kingdoms round about. And if any did not pay, there was always Morholt, the King's brother to persuade them. The man was a brute – more armour than flesh, more snarl than conversation. He so daunted the kings of Wales and Cornwall and Mann that they paid tribute year after year: twelve maidens and twelve young men. King Mark of Cornwall wept as he thought of those youngsters condemned for ever to cut peat in the bogs of Ireland.

Then up and spoke Sir Tristan of Lyonesse. "I shall fight Morholt, my lord!"

"Oh Tristan, you are like a son to me," said King Mark. "What if you should lose? Morholt would not leave one stone of Lyonesse above the crawling sea!"

"Then I shall fight him under a plain flag and keep my visor down, and no-one shall know who made the challenge!" said Sir Tristan. Mark knew

that once the bold Prince of Lyonesse had dared a venture, he would not turn back from it. So he gave Tristan a ship and sent him to Ireland to cross swords with Morholt.

Morholt's hide was tough as rhinoceros, and his strength as bottomless as the sea. Trophies of defeated men hung from his belt: a glove, a helmet, a swordhilt, a boot. Fighting him was like hacking at a tree. But at last Tristan fetched him such a blow to the head that his sword split the helmet clean across and a sliver of sword was left in Morholt's skull. He fell – an avalanche of metal and leather, webbing and chainlink.

Even in death, Morholt's thoughts were only of killing. With his last ounce of strength he pulled himself up on one elbow and pitched his spear at Tristan, piercing him behind the knee.

"You have spent your last breath in vain," said Tristan, because he was no more than grazed.

"Not so, nameless whelp!" grinned Morholt. "Do you think I won all these trophies by fighting fair? The spear is poisoned. I shall die first, but you will soon follow after me!"

Tristan had just killed the brother of the King. It was no place to stop and lick his wounds. He leapt aboard his ship. By the time he reached Cornwall, he was feverish; by the time he had reported his victory, he could barely stand. King Mark sent into every county, seeking a cure for his favourite knight, but it seemed Morholt would have his revenge after all.

"Send to Aengus," whispered Tristan. "King Aengus has a daughter called Isolde. Isolde is famous through all Ireland as a woman of

 herbs and remedies. Send for Isolde."

"I shall send, but will she come?" King Mark wondered. "To tend the

killer of her uncle?"

"She won't know it was me," said Tristan. "I fought under a plain flag and I kept my visor down."

In those days, Ireland was far across the water, and King Aengus was proud that his daughter's fame had spread so far. The princess came, with a basket of herbs and liniments, when all the doctors and priests had given up Tristan for dead. She looked him over with a piercing eye and said, "Sure, if he lives till morning, he'll live a great while after."

King Mark was away. His ministers had advised him to take a new wife, a young wife, in the hope of an heir being born to the widower King. So he never saw the princess who nursed his favourite knight. Tristan was feverish, raving and hallucinating. He saw a face, but to him it was a harpy, a fairy, a

crow, a unicorn. When, one morning, he woke to a cool pillow and the sound of birdsong, Princess Isolde was already dressed to leave, in her grass-woven cloak and straw-woven bonnet. She held up something which glittered in the sunlight. Her green eyes glittered, too.

"I took this from the wound in my uncle's head," she said, wagging the shard of metal. "One day, I thought, I shall find the sword it broke from, and be

 revenged on Morholt's killer."

Tristan looked quickly round the room.

"If you are looking for your sword, I just
threw it to the ducks in the moat below," said
Isolde, "when I found the sliver missing from its blade."

"You could have killed me while I slept."

"Yes. But it seemed wasteful to save a man's life only to cut his throat.
I shall not tell my father. He would not thank me for sparing his brother's
killer. Even so, Sir Tristan, if ever I see your face again, I shall account it the
greatest misfortune." And away she went, a long red-gold tail of hair lashing
like a whip beneath her bonnet.

King Mark returned glum and weary. He had been as far north as
Scotland, as far south as the Island of Scilly, without finding a bride who
pleased him. As he approached his castle, a goose paddled out of the moat.
From its beak hung something glistening – a fishing line? A bowstring? No.
It was a single hair – red-gold – longer than any Mark had ever seen before.

"It is an omen," he said. "I shall marry the girl who shed this hair, and
no other."

"But sire!" protested the chancellor. "The geese are migrating! This one
may have come from Norway or Finland or Iceland or Ireland!"

"Then begin searching!" declared Mark. "And scarlet gloves and a bridle to
match to the man who finds her for me."

So the knights of Cornwall and Lyonesse kissed hands with their king and
embarked on a quest. And Tristan, too, cured of his wound, kissed Mark's
hand and swore: "I shall bring you back your bride. May Heaven fail me, if I
fail my sovereign liege."

Of course he knew exactly how the hair
had come to snag in the goose's bill and

knew, too, where to look for its owner. But this he kept to himself. Wooing the woman in question would be hard enough a quest.

When Tristan arrived in Ireland, the countryside of Munster was in uproar. Ships lay burned to the keel, houses to rings of ash. A dragon was loose in Munster, and with Morholt dead there was no-one man enough to fight it. "The hand of my daughter to any knight who kills the beast!" Aengus declared.

This time, Tristan arrived in his own colours, the banner of Lyonesse standing on his stirrup. And though the beast had the hide of an elephant and feet like porcupines, though it sneezed pellets of clinker, and stank like a rotting coelacanth, it was, after all, only a dragon. It was no match for the finest knight in Lyonesse.

The look on Isolde's face was far more frightening, as Tristan stood before the throne of her father, covered in the slimy saliva of the dead dragon. She could not, in all honour, refuse to marry Tristan for he had won her fair and

square, but she drew up the edge of her cloak across her green eyes, to shut out the loathsome sight of him. "He may have won my hand, but my heart's my own!" thought Isolde.

"Take her – she is yours," said King Aengus delightedly. "She's a fortunate girl, too, for you are as fine a knight as ever wore stars or moon!"

"I do take her," said Tristan bowing, "but not for myself. My liege lord, King Mark, has vowed to have her for his queen, and it was for him that I won her."

Isolde emerged from her cloak, part relieved, part discomforted to find herself suddenly betrothed to a man she had never seen.

"Is it well, daughter?" said Aengus.

"It is well, Father," said Isolde obediently.

It was a fine political alliance, a very satisfactory outcome all in all. Only one doubt nagged at King Aengus as he watched his only daughter board the ship for Cornwall. "Take this potion," he told a maidservant carrying Isolde's chest of medicines aboard. "Make sure your mistress drinks it on her wedding eve. King Mark is old – and not as... gladsome a sight as he once was. But this liquor will guarantee Isolde looks fondly on her bridegroom. It is a love potion."

The sea was uneasy. The little ship was tipped and rolled till not a face looked east to England but it was Irish-clover green. Isolde called her maid, but her maid was too sick to come. Instead, she asked a passing sailor, "Be so kind as to fetch me the blue phial from my sea chest. It is a remedy against seasickness."

 The sailor gazed at the bewildering array of bottles and phials, and brought the bluest, which the Princess drank, thinking it to be

her home-made remedy. Grudgingly, she thrust the liquor at Tristan. "Here. This will make you feel better." He had spared her having to marry him, she had to admit. There must be some good in him.

The potion did make them feel better. Indeed, it quickly made both of them forget the heaving green sea, the pitching, groaning ship.

"You must esteem your King very highly, to win a bride for him," said Isolde.

"I swore an oath," said Tristan.

"I hope he rewards such loyalty."

"And I hope I die, sooner than see him kiss you."

"I fear I shall die of being kissed, if not by you."

"But I killed your uncle…!"

"He deserved to die. No-one liked him. He had no heart, and a man should have a heart."

"I had one, but it is lost," said Tristan.

"Have mine," said Isolde.

And though the little ship tossed its mast from side to side, Tristan and Isolde were blind to its warning finger. Their magical love was much deeper than the shallow sea which had till now separated them.

There was nothing to be done. Tristan's oath demanded that he deliver King Mark his bride, and her father's oath demanded that Isolde marry the King. But the bonds of marriage were not strong enough to keep the lovers apart.

When the maid went to the chest and realised what had happened, she dared not speak up – only watch and worry and wonder what was to be done. The lovers met as often as they could. They kissed as often as they dared. They were discreet. But the maid confided her secret to the royal seamstress. The seamstress let it slip to her husband. Her husband asked his

mother's advice and the mother gossiped of it in the Great Hall. The herald overheard, and spread the rumour far and wide.

King Mark, meanwhile, sat long and late by his hearth, jabbing at the fire with a poker. He was saddened and perplexed at his young wife's coldness. He had tried everything to make her happy. "Am I just too old to expect her love?" he asked his friend the chancellor.

"Perhaps she has already given that elsewhere," said the chancellor maliciously.

King Mark tightened his grip on the poker. "You mean she is unfaithful to me?"

"Oh Sire! Heaven forbid I should slander the Queen so! All I would say is this: be chary of young Tristan. In the greenwood. By the Sour Pool."

King Mark did not want to believe it. But once the seed of jealousy was sown, it grew to a rankness inside him. He had to be sure. He went to the little wood outside the castle walls, to a tall leafy tree whose branches overhung the Sour Pool. There he hid, silent as a sleeping owl, and heard the crack of twigs as two people approached from opposite directions.

Isolde was first to arrive. She crouched down by the water. As she reached out, she saw a face beneath her hand. Ripples fractured the face, but it was unmistakably the King's!

"My Queen!" said Tristan's voice behind her, urgent and tender.

"Ah, Sir Tristan," said Isolde, standing up abruptly. "So good of you to spare the time for these Latin lessons of ours." There was a sharp, businesslike edge to her voice. "I do so dread that my dear husband will find

out my ignorance, but in Ireland the young ladies are simply not educated so well as here."

She inclined her head ever so slightly towards the pool. Tristan knelt to wash his hands, and saw the King's face floating in the water like a summer moon.

"Madam, believe me, I shall never betray our secret, I do assure you."

Up in his tree, King Mark cursed himself for doubting his wife, for doubting noble Sir Tristan, for sinking so low in climbing so high. For months after, he would not suffer a bad word to be spoken about either of them.

But the effect of the potion held. Or if it did not, Tristan and Isolde had learned to love one another better than any magic could make them. Soon secret meetings were not enough; and they sickened of deceit. "I must have you all to myself, lady, or not at all," said Tristan, and Isolde bowed her head in submission, forfeiting a queen's crown as willingly as a chain of daisies.

They fled Cornwall for the forests of Lyonesse. There, the forest cradled them, the rocks pillowed their heads, and they had a million stars to spend. For three years they were sublimely happy.

Sleeping one morning in the last grey minutes before dawn, Tristan and Isolde dreamed of the ocean again, and of a ship with black sails, wagging its mast in warning. And when they woke, Cornish soldiers stood around them and King Mark's boot rested on Tristan's chest.

"Tristan of Lyonesse, leave this land and never return, on pain of death. Isolde of Munster, when a jewel comes loose and drops from my crown, I keep it safe by me, pouched up and out of sight of thieves. That is how I shall keep you from this day on."

South across the water from Lyonesse lies Brittany, where the exiled Tristan wept tears of bitter despair. "I shall marry no woman but Isolde," he said, letting the words drop like poison into his tankard of ale, until, like poison, he swallowed his words.

For he did marry – a Breton maiden whose name was also Isolde: Isolde-of-the-white-hands. She loved Tristan with such a sunny passion that she thought she could dispel his melancholy like a morning mist. She was so beautiful that half the princes in France were in love with her, but she set her heart on Tristan and, by sheer willpower, won him.

She won his name, she won the distant lands he could no longer enjoy. She won the title wife. But though she shone on him like an August sun, she could not thaw his soul frozen solid around the memory of Isolde of Munster. Finally his coldness extinguished her happiness, too. Theirs was a dark and frosty marriage.

"We should have killed the man before he ever set foot in Brittany!" declared her disappointed suitors, quick to sympathise and to heap criticism on the man from Lyonesse.

"I wish you had," sighed Isolde in a moment of despair.

Many years had passed since Morholt threw a poisoned spear at Tristan. The spear which pierced him in the back next day was tipped with another poison: envy. He dragged himself home to his wife's castle, and when she saw him lying there on the threshold, all her thwarted love came flooding back. Everything she could, she did to save his life, nursing him night and day. But his soul slipped away from her, out of reach, as it had always done.

At last, she bent close to his ear and whispered, "Shall I send for her to come?"

For the first time, his face brightened. "Just the sight of her would make me live," he admitted, smiling as tenderly at her as he had ever done. "But she would not come. Mark may not let her. Or her love may have died…as I am dying without her. Tell the ship's crew, if she is aboard when they return, to raise a white sail. If she is not, tell them to raise a black one."

When Isolde received the note, she gave it at once to her husband the King and said simply, "I must go to him."

He saw in her face that it was true and nodded.

Her red-gold hair blowing loose in the Channel wind was touched with grey. The hands gripping her basket of herbs set the rosemary trembling.

"Raise the white sails. You will be sure to raise the white sails!" she called to the Captain, time and time again.

"Is she coming yet?" asked Tristan for the fiftieth time.

"There is a ship on the horizon."

"Are the sails white or black?" he asked, trying to stir, trying to sit up.

"At this distance I cannot tell."

She saw how bright his eyes were at the thought of seeing Isolde of Munster, how he longed for the Irish woman with every fragment of his being. Why could he not have loved her like that: her, his rightful wife, his devoted slave? Why?

"Ah, I see now," said Isolde-of-the-white-hands. "So she would not come, after all. The sails are black as pitch."

Isolde lifted her green skirts and ran all the way from the harbour across the raw, ragged rocks, to the castle. "Is he living? Have I come in time?"

Isolde-of-the-white-hands still stood by the window, her eyes on the sea. An arm hung limp over the side of the bed, its knuckles brushing the floor.

"I'm afraid not, lady," said Tristan's wife. "My husband died this half-hour since."

But turning to relish the effect of her words, Isolde laid her white hands to her mouth. For her rival lay dead on the floor, her heart as empty of life as a birdcage left unlocked.

King Mark, when he heard of the death of Tristan and Isolde, gave orders that they be buried together in Lyonesse, side by side. And vines grew from both graves, intertwined, tendril encircling tender tendril, until it was impossible to say where one plant ended and the other began.

The Kingdom of Lyonesse no longer exists, drowned by some inexplicable oceanic grief which sank its fields and forests under five fathoms of salt water. But fishermen out in their boats, off the tip of Cornwall, say that when the sea is stormy, its church bells can still be heard tolling, as if in mourning, or ringing, as if for a wedding.

The Willow Pattern Story

Great was the power of the mandarins of old China, and great was their wealth. One such mandarin lived in a mansion two storeys high and surrounded by the blossom of peach trees.

The gardens were a paradise of pools and flowers, bridges and pavilions. Not that he did the gardening himself. Oh no. Whenever his secretary, Chang, had no letters to write or sums to calculate, he was sent into the garden to prune or dig. Chang did not complain. He loved the garden, with its golden carp, its wealth of flowers, and he soon became as excellent a gardener as he was a secretary.

But to Chang, by far the rarest bloom in the garden was the mandarin's daughter, Lotus Petal. Her father would not let her venture beyond the high walls of his gardens, for she was a great beauty, and he was saving her up, like a shiny coin in a cash box, in the hope of buying himself a rich son-in-law.

Like Chang, Lotus Petal liked to stand on the ornamental bridge and watch the golden fishes swim by below. Secretly, she loved still more to watch the sloe-black eyes of Chang.

One day, as their two reflections stood side by side in the water, Lotus
Petal said, "Oh! Did you see how that little fish swam through my heart and
then through yours? I almost felt it here in my breast. Did you feel nothing?"

Chang gripped the rail of the bridge. "Oh! How can a humble secretary
speak to the daughter of a mandarin about the love which swims around
his heart!"

Then Lotus Petal knew that Chang returned her love.

Every day they tried their best to meet in secret corners of the timber
maze or on the ornamental bridge. And when they could not be together,
they asked the birds in the garden to carry love letters scrawled on tiny
scrolls, between their tiny beaks.

Then one day Lotus Petal wrote: "Save me, Chang! My father has found a
husband for me as old as a tortoise and twice as ugly!"

All Chang's timid fears left him. Whistling up the birds, he gave them this note to carry: "Tomorrow let us stand together beneath the orange blossom and promise to love one another for ever! No one shall part us!"

Hand in hand they made their vows, which rose skyward through the sweet-smelling blossom. And who should be sitting at his upstairs window but the old mandarin. The tender words stung his ears like bees, and he leaned over his sill and blared: "Be gone, worthless Chang! Leave my house! How dare you even speak to my daughter, you low-born, penniless clod! She is promised to Ta Jin the merchant, and Ta Jin shall have her within the week!"

So, just as the willow began to shed its slender leaves, Chang was banished, and Lotus Petal's tears rippled the leaf-strewn lake, though wedding lanterns were being hung by the hundred throughout the loveless garden.

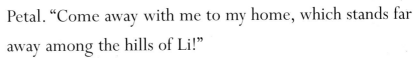

All the little birds saw her weep. Now they flew to Chang's aid. He slipped a tiny note into the bluebird's bill and the bluebird carried it to Lotus

Petal. "Come away with me to my home, which stands far away among the hills of Li!"

That night, she climbed down to him through the branches of the orange tree.

"The gates to the garden are locked, and the walls are too high to climb," said Lotus Petal. "Let's hide in the gardener's hut on the island in the centre of the lake. My father will never look for me in so foul a place. Then when he goes outside to search for us and leaves the gates unlocked, we shall get away."

So they crossed their beloved bridge hand-in-hand, and hid

all night in the gardener's hut, where earwigs massed and slugs wrote a poetry of their own on the rotten boards, in silver slime.

All next day they heard the noise of the servants searching, shaking the last leaves from the weeping willow, while the mandarin himself roamed his garden, swearing vengeance on Chang. At last both garden and house fell silent. Huddled on their island, Lotus Petal and Chang kissed and prepared to make their escape.

But as they crept out of the hut, the birds, overcome with joy at the sight of them, burst into song. A moment later, there on the bridge, barring their way stood the old mandarin, a huge whip in his hand. "There is no escape!" he shouted. "I've trapped you, faithless Chang. Prepare to die!"

It was true. There was no way off the island but across the bridge. Lotus Petal gave a cry of terror.

On and on the mandarin came, cracking his whip. "Jump, Chang!" cried Lotus Petal. "Jump with me into the water! If we cannot be together in life, at least we can be together in death!"

Up on to the rail they stepped, the whiplash cracking at their ankles, shredding silken hems. Hand in hand Chang and Lotus Petal leapt to certain death in the waters below…

Great was the power of the mandarins of old China. But greater still was the power of the gods! Looking down from the mountain tops, the gods loved Lotus Petal and Chang for their faithfulness. Just as the whipcord slashed the air where they had been standing, the gods transformed the lovers…

…into turtle-doves.

Once, twice, they circled the garden, its painted pavilions and trellised fences, its mazes, pergolas and orange groves. They swooped and soared through the ancient boughs, gathering around them a train of courtiers worthy of the Emperor of China: bluebirds, finches, swallows and thrushes. Then away they flew – out of sight and out of reach of the cruel old mandarin.

It is said they built their nest far away, among the hills of Li, and that when the sky is the blue of morning glories, the gods retell their love-story in swirling pictures of cloud-white glaze.

Certainly, potters less skilled than the gods have been honouring the lovers ever since, in the blue-and-white glaze of the Willow Pattern.

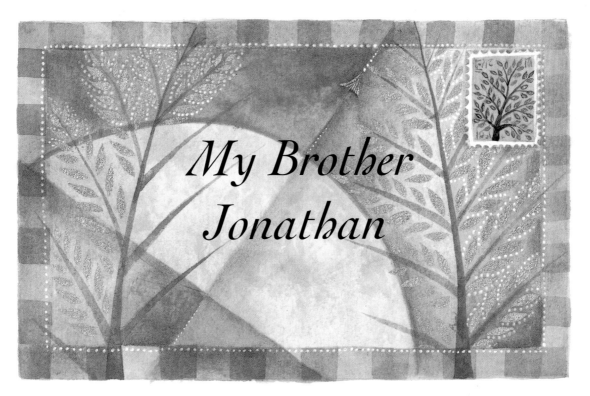

My Brother Jonathan

There stood David, hardly more than a boy, the severed head in his hand almost too heavy for him to hold. He was dressed in a shepherd's tunic and sandals – no armour, no sword or helmet – and there was a slingshot stuck into the cord of his belt. The King was impressed. Had this lad really defeated giant Goliath, champion and mascot of the Philistine army?

But if King Saul was impressed, his son Prince Jonathan was struck dumb with admiration. He thought he had never seen so marvellous a sight as David, son of Jesse, holding the dripping head of Goliath.

Plainly, after such a triumph, David-the-Giant-Killer could not be sent home to a life of minding sheep. It was quickly agreed he should stay at the King's side, eat at his table, join his circle of generals. No one was more pleased than Jonathan, for the friendship which arose between them was instant, like a bolt of lightning searing two trees together. And like two rivers flowing into each other, there could be no parting them afterwards. Jonathan gave David his own fine clothes to wear, his own sword – even his best bow.

David had a gift for music (as well as slaying giants) which made him twice over a godsend to the court of King Saul. For the never-ending war with the Philistines was draining the King. Music soothed him; the sight of David playing his harp soothed him still more.

With time, David became a great general. How the people adored this handsome young hero as he marched home at the head of a triumphant army. "Saul has killed his thousands, but David has killed his tens of thousands!" they sang. ·

Those were the words that began it. Those were the words which echoed round King Saul's head like clanging bells, that beat against his brain until he thought his skull would split. Foolishly, his ministers sent David to calm him with music.

Looking out between his fingers, Saul no longer saw comfort; he saw a rival, a conspirator, a threat. The people loved this boy, more than him. Even his own son loved David more than...

Saul picked up a spear and threw it. It thudded into the wall alongside David's head, quivering as the King was quivering with rage.

David bolted. He did not stop to ask what he had done: he just ran. Jonathan came and found him, distracted, white-faced, apologising on his father's behalf.

"Don't go!" he pleaded. "He listens to me. I can always bring him round."

"But you're his son!" said David. "You can't side with me against your own father!"

Jonathan clasped his friend's wrists and brought their faces so close that their hair touched. "My first loyalty is to you. Nothing and no one will ever be more important to me, I swear."

At dinner-time, Jonathan asked his father: "What did David do to anger you, Father? I'm sure he didn't mean to —"

"He's ambitious. He wants power. He wants my crown, that one."

"No, Father. I know David. He reveres you as God's anointed King over Israel."

The red mists of rage cleared within Saul's head, and he was pacified. David was restored to favour, and the sound of his harp brought sighs of relief from the whole royal household.

But once again the madness fell on Saul and once again Jonathan stood as buffer between them, trying to fend off disaster.

It could not last. Next time Saul threw his spear at David the tip grazed his cheek, and the hatred behind the throw grazed his very soul. He dared not even run home, but hid in the fields near the palace and waited for Jonathan to come to him, as he always came.

"He means to kill me this time," said David.

"No, no! The mood will pass." There were tears on Jonathan's lashes as he touched the graze on David's cheek. "You stay hidden here. Tomorrow morning, I'll come to this field to practise archery. If I shoot three arrows short of you, it is safe to come out: Father has seen sense. If I shoot beyond you… But it won't come to that. It won't! It mustn't." Even so, his tone was pleading rather than certain. His hand on David's arm trembled.

At dinner, Jonathan spoke up for the absent David. His eyes glowed with tenderness as he spoke of his friend. But Saul suddenly erupted from his chair. "You! You care more about that upstart traitor than your own flesh and blood! It's not natural! It's not safe! He's turned you against me! You need rescuing from a friend like that! It's time to cut you adrift from evil influences. It's time he died!"

Crouched cold and aching, weary with misery, David sat wedged in the cleft of a large boulder, awaiting Jonathan's signal. TWANG went the arrow string, and again, TWANG. The arrow fletches cut through the still air above David's head, and the arrows plummeted into the ground beyond him. Just as surely, David's heart plummeted, for it was the signal to go, to leave, to run. From this day forward, he would be the King's sworn enemy, exiled from the King's family – from the King's dear, dear son.

David waited in his hiding place until Jonathan appeared to say a final goodbye to his friend. They fell on each other's necks and wept, without any attempt to hide their feelings.

"Oh Jonathan, you've been the best friend to me a man could have. I'll never forget you."

"Oh David, I swear, when the rest of the world has turned its back on you, I shall still be your friend. You are dearer to me than my own life."

"And I swear, too, that you and I will never be enemies."

"Swear it again!" said Jonathan, laughing through his tears. "Then you must go. Father's men are out looking for you. They have orders to put you to death."

After that, Saul gave free rein to his madness. So great was his hatred for David that he expended more effort on hunting him than on fighting the war. His troops, seeing the wrong-headedness of it, deserted in droves to serve their hero, David. Soon David fielded a formidable army, and the country, already war-torn, was pitched into hideous civil war.

Just once, Jonathan was able to cross the lines of sentries and meet with

David in a wooded wilderness called Ziph. The two men regarded each other in the evening gloom. "Don't worry," said Jonathan. "My father won't find you. He has offended God, I see that, and God has withdrawn His hand from Saul's head. He means you to be King of Israel. And when you are, who'll be at your side? I will. Your faithful Jonathan. Father knows that. He keeps me by him. That's only right: I'm his son; I must stay at his side. But he knows where my heart truly lies. Remember our oath."

"I do," said David. "Friends for ever. You and yours. Me and mine."

They stood for a long time, their arms around one another, while the moon overhead looked pale for lack of blood.

The Philistines made the most of the unhappy situation in Israel. They grew in strength and mustered on Israel's borders, an unignorable threat. Saul had to break off from his obsessive war with David to confront the real enemy. He felt an emptiness behind him as though a strong wall had been demolished, exposing him to a chill wind. Had God too deserted, then? Had He too sided with David?

David was fighting Philistines elsewhere when a messenger brought the news to David – laid it at his feet like a prize. The battle on Gilboa Heights had gone against the King. Side by side, amid the spokes of smashed chariots and the carnage of defeat, Saul and Jonathan had both died. The messenger bowed low. After all, David was now King of Israel. He would surely be pleased.

David put his hands to the collar of his robe and a small, shapeless noise

welled up in his throat. He tore the robe's seams open. He fell on his knees and, scooping up dirt and dust, ground it into his hair, smeared his face with it. And all the time, the groan in his throat rose to a roar.

Eventually the rhetoric of anger abandoned him and David crouched still, small and wretched on the ground. He looked at the messenger with sightless, streaming eyes. "Oh my brother Jonathan, are you gone? You loved me more than any woman ever did. And are you gone? Well, there's an end then. To all greatness. All glory."

When David was able to think again, he asked, "Is anyone left of the house of Saul?" His officers made enquiries. The news was bleak. Of all the faces that had made up the court of King Saul, only two were left alive: one steward named Ziba and one young boy.

"The child is nothing but a cripple, my lord," the officer told him. "Dropped as a baby. Lame in both feet. His name is Mephibosheth – Prince Jonathan's son."

Ziba was fetched. David told him, "Take everything that belonged to the dead King – house, belongings, everything. They're yours. I won't

touch them, I swear."

Then Mephibosheth was hauled before King David; the boy fell clumsily on his face, terrified for his life, since he was the only surviving relative of Saul who had tried so often to kill David.

David went and raised him to his feet. He was a strange little chap, his feet all buckled, his legs undeveloped. David looked into the boy's face. Perhaps there were traces of Jonathan in those dark, frightened eyes.

"Mephibosheth, you shall have all the lands that belonged to your grandfather the King. And you shall sit at my table and share my bread, all the days of your life."

Mephibosheth blinked up at him:

"But why?"

David smiled. "Friends for ever. You and yours. Me and mine," he said, thinking aloud, remembering. "Your father and I once vowed a vow – that we would be true to each other to the ends of the earth and for all time. Well, Mephibosheth, I've lost him now. But God has left me you. And for your father's sake I mean to treat you like a prince royal…if you will be my friend."

"I will, my lord!" Mephibosheth blurted out his promise. "Me and mine. Your friend. And servant. Always."

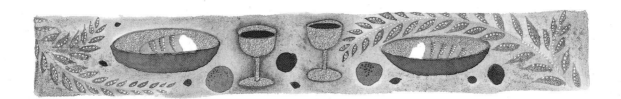

Harlequin and Columbine and Pierrot too

Little Harlequin was juggling with his heart one day, when it sprouted wings and flew away. Harlequin was left heartless.

Now, when beautiful Columbine kissed him he felt nothing.

The Doctor was sent for, who poked and prodded. But he could not find Harlequin's heart.

A Merchant tried to sell Harlequin a heart of tin, or velvet, or leather. But none were any use, because only a real heart can feel.

A Thief was sent for who had stolen many a heart. But he said, "I only steal the hearts of women. What use are they to Harlequin?"

Columbine searched high and low for Harlequin's heart, and found it singing in a tree. She caught it in a net, like a crimson butterfly, and took it back for him to wear safe inside his coat.

"Oh Columbine, I love you!" sighed Harlequin. "With all my heart!" "Oh Harlequin, I love you too," laughed Columbine. "But not as much as I love Pierrot!"

Harlequin heard a strange crack. He reached inside his coat and, sure enough, his little heart was breaking. Columbine took Pierrot by the arm and danced him down the street, and all little Harlequin could do was look up at the moon and sigh…

Solomon's Sword

*I*t *was Hester's* word against Miriam's. And Solomon had to judge between them.

The wisdom of King Solomon was renowned the world over. For legend said that Solomon had dreamed a dream, and in that dream God had offered him anything he desired.

"Give me wisdom, Lord," Solomon had said. (He must have been pretty wise already, to make such a wise wish.) And God had been so delighted by the choice that He had added all the other, lesser things Solomon might have asked for instead: wealth, fame, health, talent…

The kingdom of Judaea had thrived under the rule of this wise king, and the justice of his judgements were legendary. But secretly, Solomon would rather have spent his days writing poetry than listening to the daily squabbles which took up so much of his time.

Today it was Hester and Miriam. They fell silent on first entering the room, awed by its soaring splendour. But by the time they reached his judgement seat they were shrieking at one another again.

"He's mine, I tell you!"

"That's a lie!"

"Yours died."

"You stole him from me! You came while I was sleeping and took my boy and left me your dead one!"

The baby in question struggled and howled in the arms of Malachi, the court usher, who held him gingerly at arm's length. Malachi could not see how the matter was to be settled, but his master would know. Malachi had seen King Solomon pronounce a thousand judgements, all of them wonderfully wise. If only the child would stop crying.

"Silence in the presence of the King!" he barked, but Miriam and Hester took no notice. Solomon had to shout to make himself heard.

"Whose child is this?"

That set them off again, arguing and squabbling, their shawls slipping to uncover heads of dishevelled hair. "He's mine! Make her give him back to me!"

"She's mad. She wants to take my boy! Look at him! He looks just like me!"

But where was the good in looking for a family likeness in that little pink face screwed up with crying? Poor little mite: he put Solomon in mind of a fox cub mewing for its vixen.

"Are there any witnesses?"

"None, my lord," said Malachi.

"The baby's mine!"

"He's mine!"

"No, mine!"

"Enough!" The women started and gaped round.

"I have a solution," said Solomon.

Malachi smiled smugly: his master, who had the solution to every problem.

"Fetch a sword," said Solomon. "Since you are both so determined to have this child, let him be split between you. I shall cut him in two, and each may take a half."

Malachi's smile froze and sagged. Of course, the women deserved no better, with their raucous wailing and shouting. But the baby in his arms was such a warm, pink little thing; so frail and vulnerable! Surely the King would not… A sword was brought, nevertheless: no one disobeyed the King of Judaea.

"Lay the child on the floor, Malachi," said Solomon. "The cut must be made cleanly. There must be no argument over who has the largest portion."

The women stared at him, open-mouthed. Hester was red-cheeked, her anger boiling inside her. By contrast, Miriam was white-faced, ghost-like in her pale clothing, her hands frozen in mid-gesture as she watched the baby set down on the floor.

"Not on the carpet," said Solomon. "On the floor, or the blood will leave a stain."

Malachi did as he was told, though his fingers tangled in the fringe of the shawl and did not want to free themselves. Such a frail, pink little thing!

Solomon rose up from his throne. He took the sword hilt in both hands and stood over the baby, his feet apart. Malachi covered his face with the sleeve of his robe: he could not bear to look. He could scarcely believe…

The blade of the sword glittered with reflections: candle flames, the baby's little feet, the red of Hester's dress. The child himself fell silent, as if sensing a momentous hour in his short life. Solomon raised the sword. His eyes narrowed as he took aim on the small, wriggling target.

"STOP!"

Solomon looked up at Miriam, vexation on his face, as if he wanted to get the business over and done with.

"Let her have him," said Miriam. Her face held all of the agonies ever suffered since the beginning of the world. "Let her have him. Only don't kill him. Not my boy... I mean to say... He's hers. He's Hester's. Hester can have him. Only don't kill him. I'm begging you, my lord King." She slumped to the ground, hands reaching first towards the wriggling baby, then drawing back against her stomach. "Let him live. I withdraw my claim."

Hester drew her lips inside her mouth, in a grin of grim satisfaction.

Solomon whirled the sword once in the air...then stood it down, propped against his judgement seat. He bent down, picked up the baby boy and kissed him on his nose.

"Now I know who is your mother, don't I, little fellow?" he said, and all the harshness had gone from his voice, all the violence. "Only Miriam loved you with the love of a mother. Only Miriam cared more about you than herself." The knuckle of his forefinger stroked the velvety cheek, then he laid the baby in the arms of Miriam. She knelt cradling him, rocking to and fro, peering to see her boy through eyes too full of tears.

"Shall I arrest this one?" asked Malachi hotly, grabbing Hester's arm. "She's perjured herself and stolen another woman's child. She must at least be flogged!"

Solomon waved a hand in reproof. Malachi noticed that the royal hand was actually trembling. "Malachi, Malachi. Has she not lost a child? What torturer could inflict a worse punishment than that?" he asked.

Then he wiped the palms of his hands down the gorgeous fabric of his poppy-red robe and went to write poetry in the small room behind the great Hall of Judgement.

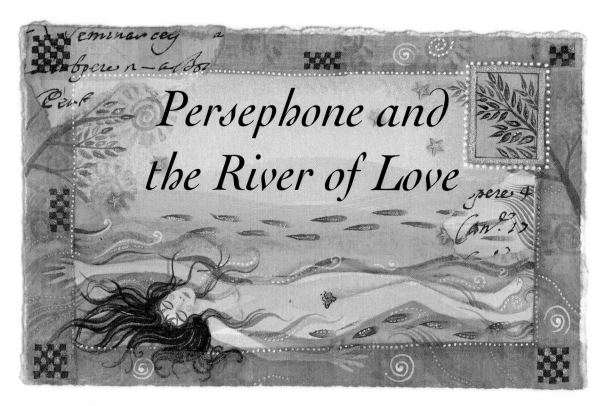

Persephone and the River of Love

The sun was hot. Arethusa went down to the river and swam. She felt the current wash her clean as she lay, eyes closed, floating face-up to the blue summer sky. Her hair spread wide.

"I love you, Arethusa," whispered the white water washing by her ears.

"Oh!" Arethusa swam for the bank. As she pulled herself ashore, the water seemed to drag on her, pulling her back, but she broke free, took to her feet and ran.

Behind her, though, the River Alpheus pulled itself from between its banks and came after her. Arethusa screamed and ran faster. "I'm too young to marry!" she cried, but still the river gave chase. Her freedom was far too dear to give up! Besides, she had never pictured herself as the bride of a river! She fled across fields and through woods, with the river following behind her like a blue train to her dress. For having held Arethusa in his arms once, Alpheus was deep, deeply in love.

Looking down from Heaven, the goddess Venus saw Arethusa running away, and took pity on the girl. One moment Arethusa could feel the sweat on her face as she ran, the next she felt both sweat and face turn to water, and flinging up her hands, she saw them too turn to spray. She was a fountain, and her blowy waterdrops hid her female form like a fog hiding a tree.

Up and down, in and out Alpheus flowed, looking for Arethusa. Just as he was about to give up, a breeze shifted the misty spray, and there she stood: "Arethusa!"

So away ran watery Arethusa, (no more than a brook, in comparison with the mighty Alpheus), skipping over the stony ground, as she searched for a hiding-place. At last she glimpsed a dark crevice between two rocks, a bolt hole, and wriggling into it, found herself falling, falling downwards. Her watery body somersaulted down before splashing onto the marble floor of the Underworld itself.

Startled wraiths blinked their hollow eyes at her. Ghosts drew back against the wall as she passed. Through halls heaving with hosts of ghosts she hurried. The whispering of shoals of souls was louder than any river. So many dead. She had never realised that so many people had died and left the sunlit world for this realm of dreary darkness!

At length she flowed to the very centre of the kingdom, into a hall with soaring black pillars hung with sable tapestries. On a throne of ebony sat Hades, God of the Underworld, and beside him a mortal. This was no ghost, but a living girl, wearing a crown of wilting flowers. Hades' hand gripped the girl's wrist, forbidding her to leave.

Glimpsing the glitter of free flowing water, the girl snatched the flowers from her hair and threw them into Arethusa's stream. "Please! Please! Carry these to my mother, and tell her where I am! Say 'Hades has Persephone, Hades has kidnapped Persephone!'"

The angry god beside her tried to snatch the flowers back, but Arethusa tumbled out of the throne-room and on through the dark galleries. She feared she would never find a way out until, seeing a diamond of yellow high above, she forced her way up through a tiny crevice and into the sunlight.

Warmth! Life! Sunshine! The amorous Alpheus was forgotten. Now Arethusa's only thought was to find that poor girl's mother. That someone living should be trapped in that fearful Land of Death! It did not bear thinking of. So scurrying over pebbles and goat tracks, she scoured the autumn countryside until at last she found a glade where a woman sat crying.

This was not any ordinary woman, but a goddess crowned with flowers. Her clothes were powdery with pollen and harvest dust and she wept inconsolably. "Oh where is my daughter? My little Persephone?"

It was Demeter, Goddess of all Growing Things. All around her lay the wreckage of summer, a dishevelled misery of trees all weeping away their leaves in sympathy.

"Your daughter is in the Underworld!" called Arethusa, her voice no more than a watery whisper. Casting the chaplet of flowers at Demeter's feet, she called as loudly as she could, "Hades is holding her prisoner! He wants her for his bride!"

The goddess sprang to her feet, "Thank you!" – suddenly hopeful of finding her missing daughter. Uphill she ran, where watery Arethusa could not follow, and hammered at the gates of Olympus. "Zeus! Oh, Zeus! Father of Gods and Ruler of the Earth! Hades has stolen my daughter away! Make him give her back! Make him give Persephone back!"

The voice of the all-powerful Zeus rumbled like thunder around the hill. "Does Hades not deserve a little happiness? His lot is a hard one. Must he languish lonely in that terrible territory of Dark? Shall he not have a wife to keep him company?"

"If he wanted a wife, he should have wooed her, not stolen her!" cried Demeter. "If you don't command him to let her go, I shan't twine the vines or brush the tresses of the trees! Without a daughter, what do I care if the world wizens and dies?"

Zeus was moved; he pitied Demeter. He was alarmed, too. The world would decay into a desert without Demeter to tend its teeming gardens and farms. There again, Hades' feelings had to be considered…

Zeus summoned Hermes, his winged messenger. "Speed to the Underworld and tell Hades he must give back Persephone to the upper world…unless, of course, she is willing to stay…or unless she has accepted his hospitality."

'Accepted his hospitality'? That could mean anything: a cup of wine, a bite of bread… Arethusa saw mother and messenger running downhill, down towards the Underworld. Water runs easily downhill, and now watery Arethusa could outrun them.

She had to know what became of poor Persephone!

"Hurry!" Demeter urged the winged messenger. "Hades will try and trick her, I know him!"

She was not wrong. With every passing hour, Hades summoned some new deliciousness to tempt his prisoner with. "Strawberries fetched from the Fields of Elysium, my dear! Truffles from the black earth above us! Won't you taste, lady? You must be hungry."

And she was. Persephone was famished. For three days she had refused every plate, every cup – too frightened at first to eat, then too miserable. But at last, when Hades left a sprinkling of pomegranate seeds on the table, she picked them up almost without thinking.

"Stop!" It was Hermes, hovering on winged sandals.

A pang of guilty fear crossed Hades' face, as he half rose from his throne. "She's eaten my food. She's mine now! You can't take her from me!"

"We shall see about that." Hermes unfolded Persephone's little fingers one by one. Six seeds still lay in her palm. She stared at him aghast.

"What have I done?" she asked. "I didn't know!"

"Shame on you, Hades. Could you not win a bride for yourself except by kidnap and trickery?"

"Trickery?" echoed Persephone, fresh tears in her eyes.

"How else could I win her, eh?" Hades answered the winged messenger. "Look at her! She's lovely! She's perfection. Do you think she would have come if I'd asked her? To this gloomy pit where the sun never shines and nothing grows but moss and mold? To lighten the life of a crusty old tyrant like me? Never!"

"You could have tried, at least!" whispered Persephone.

Of twelve pomegranate seeds, she had eaten six, and yet it was enough to seal her fate.

Watching aghast through her tiny spyhole, Arethusa barely noticed the geyser of grey-green water forcing its way out of the ground nearby. Alpheus, in following his love, had also plunged underground. Now he re-emerged, forcing his great mass through a crevice, like a crocodile through the eye of a needle. His mighty waters rushed towards her.

To his delight and astonishment, Arethusa did not run away. On the contrary, she spilled herself against him, into his reaching, grey-green arms, After all, had he not braved the fearful Underworld out of love for her? And having seen what she had seen down there and compared her fate with that of Persephone, there was nothing she wanted more now than love and sunlight and the closeness of another living being.

Stream and river intermingled and flowed onwards: bubbling rapids creamy with spray, like a wedding.

As for Demeter, she still threatened to lay waste the world if her daughter

did not come back to her. So Zeus, in his wisdom, made a judgement which changed both Upper and Lower World for ever. Because Persephone had eaten six of the twelve pomegranate seeds (he said) she must stay six months of the year in the Halls of Hades, easing his loneliness, singing to his minor, melancholy music. For the other six months of the year, she could return to her mother, helping her twine the vines and brush out the green tresses of the trees.

There was always grief while she was gone. Demeter would neglect her work and the trees weep away their leaves in sympathy. But they both had springtime to look forward to, when mother and daughter were reunited.

And in time Persephone came to love her half-year husband as dearly as her six-month mother, because his delight in her never waned. In his awkward, tongue-tied way, he loved her with the monumental, unchanging love only a god can feel. Occasionally, laughter could even be heard rising out of the darkness – deep booming guffaws and light, girlish laughter like the sound of underground rivers or subterranean waterfalls.

The Death of Death

Jack's old mother lay on the bed, her face as white as her hair, her hair as white as the pillow. When he held her hand, the pulse was fainter than the tick of the clock. She smiled at him – a flicker of a smile.

"Reckon I'll not see morning, Jack. You've been a good son to me, none better. So kiss me goodbye and I'll sleep now."

"Now, Mother, you're not to go talking like that," said Jack, his throat clogged and painful. He remembered his mother turning from the stove to greet him as he came home from school. He remembered how his mother had sung to make him sleep, tickled him to make him laugh, read to him till the room rang with stories, listened to all his workaday woes. He remembered birthdays, picnics and outings. He knew no one in the world could cook pancakes like hers; how no one in the world could make him feel so loved, so tall, so special.

"You've many good years in you yet, Mother," said Jack, "and I'm not ready to part from you. So don't you go talking of Death yet awhile."

"Talk of him or no, he'll come all the same," said the old lady. "I hear his footsteps now." And her eyelids flickered closed.

Jack jumped up from the bedside. It was true, the sound of felt boots was scuffing on the cobbles, coming closer and closer. The lock rattled, and the latch lifted. So did the hairs on Jack's neck. He whipped open the door, and was confronted by a tall stranger dressed all in black. A high tricorn hat cast the face into shadow, but he saw that it was very pale, with sunken cheeks and lips of the same parchment yellow as the skin.

"Not so fast!" cried Jack, as the stranger made to step round him.

At the first blow, the stranger reeled back against the wall and looked Jack in the face — a look of startled bewilderment. At the second blow he dropped down on one knee. Jack put his foot to the stranger's chest and pushed him backwards through the door, shutting it quickly, so that it thudded against something, and there was a third cry of pain.

"Not today, thank you, Mr Death!" said Jack triumphantly, panting hard, using his shoulder to barricade the door.

Silence. When he peeped through the window, there was no sign of anyone – only a trail of blood leading away towards Dark Alley.

Behind him, his mother sat up in bed. "What's for tea, Jack?" she asked, her night cap jaunty over one ear.

Jack could hardly believe his own daring. He had killed Death and saved his old mother! Imagine! No more death! Jack would go down in history as a hero of the human race: the boy who killed Death!

Such a triumph warranted a celebration. He would roast a chicken for his dear old mother. It would help build up her strength. Tomorrow the news would have spread, and the whole county would be feting him, with banquets and medals and rewards of money and land! How proud his mother would be of her clever Jack!

So Jack went to the hen-house and cornered the fattest old chicken of all, and grabbed it by its throat.

The creature had a neck like a steel hawser! Jack burned the palms of his hands trying to wring it. He blunted his penknife trying to stab it. He took the teeth off his saw trying to saw it. Afterwards the chicken only hopped down, looked at him reproachfully with its balding head on one side, and strutted away.

It was a bitter cold day for the time of year. Jack's hands were red raw by the time he gave up his struggle with the chicken.

He should at least go and light the stove, to keep his old mother warm. So first he went down to the edge of the forest to cut fuel for the fire.

"It must be colder than I knew," thought Jack. "This trunk is frozen solid. It just won't cut." In fact he had to give up chopping and grub up a whole sapling and carry it back to the house. Even then the thing would not burn. Too green. "See to the stove, Mother, and bake us some bread," he said bad-temperedly, and stamped out of the house again, carrying his fishing rod.

He went to the river to catch a fish for supper – caught one, too! – a lovely brown-speckled trout which he lifted ashore in a net. But when he hit it with a stick to kill it, it only bounced – boing! – like a rubber ball right back into the river. Jack howled with frustration.

By this time, he was getting seriously hungry. He and his mother had to eat something, even if it was not a celebratory banquet. So he went to the orchard with a basket, to pick the last of the summer's fruit.

But the apples on the apple tree refused to be picked. Though he swung on them with all his weight, the stems just would not snap. The tree slapped him – it slapped him! – full in the face, so that he sat down yelping with pain and frustration.

His own noise, however, was drowned out by a terrible caterwauling. In the lean-to, where he stored his grain ready for winter, a veritable army of rats and mice were chewing their way through the hessian sacks, scattering the grain about, in waves of grey-black fury. The poor old tabby cat pounced and pawed, but it had clearly lost the knack of mousing. Although Jack set about the rodents with rake and flail, they devoured all his winter provisions before his very eyes.

Ravenous and enraged, Jack went back into the house. To his disgust, his mother, far from baking them some bread, was still lying on the bed.

She signalled him to come closer. Her face was still horribly pale. "Perhaps I only injured Death," thought Jack. "I'd better go and finish him off," and he took down his hunting gun and turned towards the door.

"Oh Jack, Jack, where are you going?" asked his mother.

"In to Dark Alley. To finish the job I started," said Jack grimly.

"Oh Jack, Jack, what have you done?" asked his mother, her voice very frail.

"I killed Death, Ma. I killed him for you – at least I think I have. He won't come sniffing round here again, poking his nose in where it isn't wanted!"

His old mother sank down among the pillows. "Oh Jack, Jack, I feared as much. I thought this morning I was bound for the peace and quiet of my grave. But it seems to me a door has closed since then. Son, son, you are a foolish boy!"

"I only did it out of love of you, Ma!" protested Jack. "How could I ever

get by without you? I had to kill him!!"

"But did you kill Pain, Jack? And did you kill Sorrow?" said his old mother, taking his hand in hers. "There's a place for Death in the world, as much as the next man. Or how will the crops be reaped or the trees felled?"

Jack stared at her and thought of the orchard and of the forest and the hen-house and the river.

"How will you keep the world from growing old all over? Or make room for the newborn? How will the weary rest? You can't be rid of Death, Jack, unless you can first be rid of Pain and War and Hunger and Old Age and Weariness and Sickness and all the things that make people crave him like a good night's sleep. Oh Jack, Jack, the world won't forgive you if you have killed Death!"

"But Mother, I thought –"

"No, you didn't, son. If only you had." She squeezed his hand. "Foolish boy. Dear, dear, darling boy. How I'll miss you while we're apart. But do you really suppose I'm scared of that old ragamuffin Death? I was quite looking forward to meeting him. Such an interesting fellow, he must be, after all…"

Out of the house ran Jack, pausing only to hug his mother close and kiss her on the forehead. He sprinted on his toes across the yard and down the street towards Dark Alley all stuffed with shadow. The alley rang with emptiness. No corpse, no cloak, no Death. Jack found nothing but a few drops of blue-black blood the colour of a night sky.

Jack cupped his hands to his mouth and spun round. "Are you well, Death? Are you alive?" he called.

The dead leaves falling from the apple trees rattled along the street, hissing. The plums plopped down, soft and rotting from the plum trees with a noise like blood dripping. "Alive and ticking," said the clock on the church tower. "Alive and picking," said the sexton clearing weeds from round the graves. "Alive and kicking," clacked the door of Jack's cottage, banging in the wind.

As Jack turned, he saw an old lady at the far end of the street. She was leaning heavily on the arm of a tall, cloaked figure in a high tricorn hat; their two heads bent close together, as if sharing secrets.

Jack did not go after them. Instead, he sat down within the church lychgate. Once or twice, he wiped his eyes with the sleeve of his shirt; it would not do for a big lad like him to be seen crying... "I'll go home and tell Mother what a terrible day... No, no." For a moment he had almost forgotten: he was on his own now.

Ramming his hands between his knees, rocking forward and back, Jack gave himself up to weeping. There is a right and proper time for tears, as well as Death, after all. And Love doesn't end with Death. It just changes into something a little lonelier.

Romeo and Juliet

At the beginning, it was all gaudy colours and flags, sunlight too bright for the eyes, pushing crowds and music and too much wine. Romeo was in love, but then Romeo was always in love. Young men cannot help it. They are either fighting, or swooning with passion.

The older ones ought to know better, but it was not so in Verona. Members of the Capulet family feuded with the Montagues whether they were sixteen or sixty: spitting, throwing insults, fighting in the street. The Prince lost all patience with them. Finally, he forbad street fighting on pain of banishment. Still the hatred went on simmering in the summer heat, like a bad smell. No one remembered why the two clans hated each other; no one cared either. Montagues were born hating Capulets, and Capulets were born hating Montagues.

Poor Romeo Montague, then, to fall in love with Juliet Capulet!

He and his foolish friends had dared each other to gate-crash a masked ball at the Capulet house. Romeo glimpsed Juliet's face – and that was that. The rest of the hot world melted away. There were just the two of them, looking at each other. Falling in love.

While Romeo sighed and wrote poetry, Juliet took a more practical line. She sent her old nursemaid with a message to Romeo: I love you. I'll marry you. Meet me at the cell of Friar Laurence if you want us to be married.

The Friar thought at first that it was just a childhood infatuation – told them they were far too young to be talking of making everlasting vows. But he soon saw that he was wrong. These two children were all in all to one another. Romeo's hatred for the Capulets had shrivelled to nothing. And they were so happy! Juliet's face shone as though she had swallowed the sun.

Friar Laurence allowed himself be persuaded. He saw that they could not be separated, so he joined them, in marriage. Besides, he told himself that this love-match might just put an end to the Capulet-Montague feud once and for all.

Naturally, the couple would not be able to tell anyone they were married – not right away. The announcement had to be nicely judged, if their mothers

and fathers were not to rage and fume and disinherit them. "Keep it secret for now," said the Friar. "Wait until I can break the news tactfully."

Then, like a bridal cake that's stood too long in the sun, all the joy started to crumble.

On his way back from his secret wedding, Romeo met up with his best friend Mercutio. The two of them ran into Benvolio and Tybalt. Tybalt Capulet! Juliet's own cousin! Well, naturally Tybalt goaded his old enemies like a bullfighter pricking at a bull, but Romeo took no notice – kept trying to explain that he no longer had any quarrel with the Capulets. But because he could not say why, the other boys gawked at him in disbelief. What? Had Romeo turned coward? Was he too scared to fight? The town square was as hot as a bread oven. Tempers flared.

"I'll fight you, if Romeo won't!" Mercutio shouted at Tybalt. Then the swords were out and Romeo was trying to come between them. He grabbed hold of Mercutio. Tybalt seized his chance and made a thrust under Romeo's arm. And suddenly Mercutio was dying – cursing all Montagues and Capulets and dying.

If ever a curse struck home, that one did. Romeo snatched up his friend's sword and drove it into Tybalt's heart.

For the crime of disobeying the Prince's edict, and for killing Tybalt, Romeo was banished from Verona. Banished, on pain of death.

Romeo ran to old Friar Laurence beating his head against the walls till it bled. He was deaf to all reason; his life was over, he said. What was the pain

of death in comparison with the pain of being parted from Juliet? Laurence had to take him by the ears to shake sense into him. "While there's life there's hope, boy! While there's life, there's hope!"

It was agreed that Romeo should leave the city before morning, go to Mantua and wait there for news. Either Juliet could join him there or, when the Prince's temper cooled, Romeo might be able to return. That left Romeo just one night to spend with his bride before he left Verona.

In the meantime, of course, Juliet had heard

the news; that her beloved cousin was dead —
killed by Romeo. When Romeo came
clambering over the rail of her balcony, she
raged at him — struck out at him with feet and
fists: "Tybalt was like a brother to me! How
could you, you murderer! I hate you!" Then
he caught hold of her wrists, and she keeled
in against his chest, and they kissed. And there
was no more talk of hate.

Romeo stayed till the dawn chorus spilled
in at the window, then they kissed, their lips
still pillow-warm, and Romeo climbed down
and rode away to Mantua. He promised to
send for Juliet as soon as he had found work and somewhere to live.

That was when Juliet's parents burst in on her, one hand upraised at the
window, gazing out…at nothing. They had good news, they said. They had
decided to blot out the sadness of Tybalt's death with a far happier family
event. Juliet was to be married!

Still tearful and trembling, from saying goodbye to her husband, Juliet
learned that she was betrothed to no less a person than the Count Paris.

She tried to refuse, of course. Her father was enraged by her tears and
pleas. He threatened to disown her if she said one more word against the
idea. She would be married next morning, like it or not.

Naturally, she ran to Friar Laurence. Naturally he said he would help.
"While there's life there's hope!" he told her. While there's life there's hope.

Now, within his religious order, Friar Laurence was an apothecary. His
great talent lay in mixing potions and remedies from simple herbs and
minerals. So he made up a potion intended to save Juliet from marrying

the Count. The liquor would rob Juliet of all signs of life – make her look dead. It was a powerful, fearful concoction, but Juliet took it as eagerly as a cordial of strawberries.

As soon as she was gone, Laurence sat down and wrote to Romeo in Mantua, explaining the plan. Juliet would escape marriage to the Count Paris by pretending to die. She would be buried by her grieving family in the family vault, and it was there that Romeo should come – (preferably before Juliet woke and found herself alone among all the skeletons and spiders' webs). They could steal away together, and make a new life for themselves; not the ideal outcome, perhaps, but where there's life…

According to plan, brave Juliet drank the potion and went to sleep – so deep a sleep it was as if she had sunk to the bottom of the deepest ocean. When her nursemaid and mother came to wake her – "Wake up, Juliet! This is your wedding day!" – they found her pale as cuttleshell, cold as deep water.

While they wept and wailed, Friar Laurence smiled to himself, thinking how happy they would be one day, when they knew the truth. He knew Juliet was not dead at all, and by nightfall she would be with her true husband, with her Romeo.

But the letter never reached its destination. Accidents happen. Letters get lost. Letters get delayed. Far away in Mantua, Romeo heard tell not of Laurence's plan but of Juliet's sudden death.

He rode back mad with grief, back to the cemetery in Verona, stopping on the way only long enough to buy a phial of poison. Count Paris was loitering there, mourning in good faith his almost-bride. Romeo ran him through without a second thought.

Then he walked down into the vault, footsteps gritty on the dusty stairs.

Juliet was still sleeping. Thanks to the Friar's marvellous potion, she looked stone dead. So Romeo took out his phial of poison and drank it down

with never a pause for thought.

Meanwhile the effects of the sleeping draft were wearing off and Juliet woke to find Romeo beside her, exactly according to plan. "Romeo? Wake up, my love! You fell asleep waiting for me. Wake up, my dearest."

But when she touched him, he was cold. Cold as death.

So she took his dagger and drove it in under her breastbone. No weeping or wailing. Just a blood-filled kiss and then silence, but for the scuffling of rats.

Friar Laurence found them.

When their parents saw the bodies, the feud between Capulet and Montague was washed away in a flood of tears. They had too much in common to go on hating each other. But no one was glad. The darkness and horror of that stony place bore down on them, and they felt only the cold, the bone-chilling cold.

Heat at the beginning, cold at the end.

Or perhaps Heaven was hung with banners to welcome Juliet and her Romeo. Perhaps the streets of Heaven are always warm and gaudy with laughing crowds, cheering at the sight of true lovers reunited for ever.

Love's Palace

Shah Jehan had many wives, as was the way of Mogul emperors. But he had only one love, and that was Mumtaz Mahal. She was as lovely as a star, and he thought that, like the stars, she would shine for ever. Then one day the starlight in Mahal's eyes went out; she died in his arms, and he thought that everlasting night had swallowed him.

Crying did nothing, because tears would not bring her back. Anger did nothing, because raging would not bring her back. When the wan, waning Moon rose overhead, he cursed it, because the Moon would wax full again and Mahal would not. Why must everyone die? Why, the merest mud bricks drying in the brickfield outlasted the hands which made them!

Then it came to him – how Mahal's beauty could live for ever. Shah Jehan began to build.

"Are you building me a palace?" asked his greedy son, Aurangzeb.

"Are you building a temple to God?" asked his dear son, Shikoh.

But the building which rose out of the dust was larger and lovelier than any temple or palace. It seemed to float above the ground, and the four rivers

which met at its base were like the four rivers which meet at the heart of Paradise. Its white marble walls were inlaid with exquisite patterns of coloured gemstones. When the waxing moon rose over the Taj Mahal, it seemed no more than the finishing touch to a work of perfection. Quite simply, Shah Jehan had built the most beautiful monument in the world. Nowhere smaller could have housed his love for Mumtaz Mahal. Nothing less could have expressed his inexpressible grief.

There was worse grief to come. Shah Jehan's son Aurangzeb deposed his father as emperor and imprisoned him. He put to death Shikoh, and wrought havoc on Agra and all its empire.

But from his prison window in the Red Fort, Jehan was still able to see the Taj Mahal. Its windows winked at him in the sunlight. Its gem-studded dome throbbed like a heartbeat in the livid sunsets. Its serenity soothed his poor heart. It spoke to him of love, just as Mumtaz Mahal had done. It spoke to him of Paradise.

And a dying man who glimpses Paradise has no cause to fear. A building endures longer than a man. Soon Jehan, like Mahal was dead. But because of the Taj Mahal, their love is remembered, even now. And even now, lovers who watch the waxing moon rise over the Taj Mahal, feel the sad world crumble into light and glimpse the essence of true love.

More About the Stories

The First Family

This myth from the island of Madagascar in the Indian Ocean is of the 'taboo' kind which explains which relationships are right and proper within a closed society. It points up the different kinds of emotion, all equally strong, covered by that one vague word: Love.

Antony and Cleopatra

When in 1607, William Shakespeare wrote this, his most passionate play, he drew on the ancient writings of Plutarch who was attempting to record historical fact.

Before her love affair with Antony, Cleopatra had also won the affections of his predecessor, Julius Caesar, smuggling herself into his presence wrapped in a carpet.

Hero and Leander

The story of Hero and Leander was told by the ancient Greeks. The stretch of water then called the Hellespont (now the Dardenelles) was named after a mythical princess, Helle, who fell from the back of a flying, winged, golden ram (later Jason's Golden Fleece) and drowned.

Nineteenth century poet Lord Byron boasted that, like Leander, he had succeeded in swimming the Hellespont from shore to shore.

Unforgivable

This is probably the best known folktale in Wales. But this rendering was only put about in the 1790s, by a canny resident of Beth Kellarth. The publican of the Royal Goat Inn knew the old story, inserted the dog's name and Prince Llewellyn for local interest, and built a cairn of stones with the help of the parish clerk. The Royal Goat thrived, as tourists swarmed to the town, soon renamed Beth Gelert (Gelert's Bed), to stand and weep beside the cairn. They still do. No one knows whether somewhere, at some time, a real dog did save a real baby.

Tristan and Isolde

Tristan and Isolde (or Iseult) is an Irish/Celtic legend which has given rise to operas, literature and poetry throughout Europe. Thomas Malory incorporated it into his telling of the King Arthur legend, but it existed separately long before then – a whole cycle of stories called the Ulster Cycle, but no complete version of this any longer exists. The lovers are forerunners of Lancelot and Guinevere, and they have their roots in the even older Irish story of Deirdre and Noisi.

The Willow Pattern Story

In the 18th Century, there was a craze in the West for all things Chinese, and potters such as Thomas Turner began to produce crockery with pseudo-Chinese designs on it. This is when the Willow Pattern was invented. Sadly it has no genuine Chinese myth behind it, and there is no 'correct' interpretation of the famous blue-and-white pattern. Many stories have been invented, however, to explain the figures and buildings, plants and birds.

My Brother Jonathan
"thy love to me was wonderful, passing the love of women."

So runs David's lament for Jonathan, in the Old Testament Book of Samuel. After Saul's death, David (author of the Psalms and held to be an ancestor of Jesus) became the second King of Israel from roughly 1000-960BC.

Harlequin and Columbine and Pierrot too

Arlecchino and Columbina were characters in Italian knockabout theatrical comedies of the 16th Century. From Italy they migrated to French, then to English pantomime. The same characters appeared in every play, and the slapstick was more important than any plot. This scene is intended to capture the blithe, bitter-sweet mood of Harlequin and Columbine's surreal world.

Solomon's Wisdom
"The wisdom of God was in him, to render judgement."

This is the biblical conclusion, in the Book of Kings, to the story of Solomon and the baby. The incident would have happened in about 950BC. Interestingly the same story appears in 14th-century Chinese literature, when the baby is placed in a chalk circle and the women told to win him in a tug of war. Solomon, son of David, was builder of the First Temple in Jerusalem and possible author of the Song of Songs, another of the books in the Old Testament and one rich in images of love.

Persephone and the River of Love

The Greek myth of Persephone and Demeter is much better known than the little love story within it, of Alpheus and Arethusa. Their myth came about as a way of explaining the strange route of the Alpheus, largest river of southern Greece, which disappears underground for many miles before resurfacing into the light of day. Arethusa's fountain is also a famous landmark – but not on the Greek mainland. It waters the little island of Delos, near Syracuse.

The Death of Death

This tale is one of a wealth of English 'Jack' stories in which the hero usually does something stupid at the outset but redeems his mistake by some act of bravery, cunning or quick-wittedness.

Romeo and Juliet

This most famous love story of all first appeared in the Novellino (Little Stories) of Masuccio Salernitano (1476), retold in English by Arthur Brooke in 1567. It is this version on which Shakespeare based his play in 1596. Since then, operas, ballets, films and a musical (West Side Story) have delighted in retelling the story.

Verona prides itself on being the 'real-life' home of Romeo and Juliet, but they may never have existed.

Love's Palace

The city of Agra stands on the River Jumna in India and was the capital of the Mogul empire in the 17th Century. Mumtaz Mahal died aged 38 and her mausoleum was built between 1631-1653 by workmen from as far afield as Italy and Turkey. The gems studding its walls and domes have all been stolen, but the beautiful stonework remains. It is thought Shah Jehan may have styled the Taj Mahal on descriptions of Paradise given in the Koran. So his efforts may not have been for his wife alone, but also an act of worship to his God.